BUGS BUNNY™
and the Pink Flamingos

By GINA INGOGLIA
Illustrated by JOHN COSTANZA

A GOLDEN BOOK · NEW YORK
Western Publishing Company, Inc., Racine, Wisconsin 53404

Bugs Bunny was walking down the street, eating a carrot and singing a song.

"Springtime is here..." he sang, "the
birdies are chirpin'...the flowers are bloomin'..."
"Hi, Bugs," said a voice. It was Elmer Fudd.

"What's up, doc?" Bugs asked Elmer. "Getting your vegetable garden ready for spring?"

Elmer sighed. "The birds keep eating up all the seeds."

"That's a shame," said Bugs.

Just then, along came some of their friends.

Daffy was pushing a heavy lawn mower.

"Shouldn't you be doing that on the *grass*?" asked Bugs.

"I just got it fixed at the repair shop," said Daffy. "Now I have to go home and mow the lawn. I hate that job."

"I've got to plant these petunias," said Porky. "They're my favorite flower," he added, smiling at Petunia Pig. "But all that bending over wears me out."

"I hate to say it, pal," said Bugs, "but if you exercised more, you'd bend over better."

"Well, I've got to get going," said Petunia. "My fence needs painting."

She looked at Bugs. "You're lucky you live in a rabbit hole," she said. "You don't have spring chores."

"Right!" said Porky and Daffy.

"Listen," said Bugs. "I have an idea. I could use a little pocket money. I'll go into the gardening business and do all your spring chores for you. What do you say?"

"I say *yes*!" said Petunia.

"Me, too!" said Daffy and Porky.

"What about you, Elmer?" asked Bugs.

"No, thanks, Bugs," said Elmer. "I love taking care of my vegetable garden."

The next morning Bugs started
his gardening business.

He planted Porky's flowers, and
he watered them every day.

He painted Petunia's fence.

And he took good care of Daffy's lawn.

"You're doing such a great job, Bugs," said Petunia.
"You really have a green thumb."
"My grass never looked better," said Daffy.

"I wish I could say the same for my vegetable garden," said Elmer. "The birds are eating the seeds as fast as I plant them."

"Our picnics won't be the same without Elmer's corn on the cob," said Porky with a sigh.

"Or his carrots," said Bugs. "Don't forget about the carrots!"

That afternoon Bugs saw a sign outside the hardware store.

"Wow," he said, running inside. "Those plastic pink flamingos give me an idea!

"How many flamingos are left?" Bugs asked.

"Twenty," said the shopkeeper.

"Perfect!" said Bugs. "Five for Daffy, five for Porky, five for Petunia, and five for me." He paid for the birds and dashed to the door. "I'll be right back for them."

In a few minutes Bugs was back
with Porky, Petunia, and Daffy.
   "Here," said Bugs, piling five
flamingos into Daffy's arms. "I want you
to carry a few things for me.

   "Hold out your arms, Porky," said Bugs.
"Five flamingos for you.

"And, Petunia," he added, "five for you."
"Aren't you going to carry some, Bugs?"
asked Petunia.

"Of course," said Bugs.
"Five for me. And I'll lead the way.

"Follow me," said Bugs. "It's only a few blocks from here."

"A few *blocks*?!" groaned Porky. "I don't think I can carry all this."

"Sure you can," said Bugs. "We'll be there before you know it."

"Watch out, Daffy," said Petunia. "You're poking me."

"Sorry," said Daffy, dropping a flamingo.

Porky bumped into Daffy, and more flamingos fell to the sidewalk.

"Don't worry," said Bugs. "It won't be long now."

Bugs stopped in front of Elmer's house.

"Hi," Elmer said. "What are you doing with all those pink flamingos?"

"A good question," said Porky.

"No time for talk," said Bugs. "Follow me."

They lugged the birds behind Elmer's house.

"Start sticking the flamingos all over Elmer's vegetable garden," said Bugs.

When they were finished, Elmer looked at his yard. "This is pretty strange," he said.

"Now," said Bugs, "let's hide behind that tree."

As soon as they were out of sight they heard a loud chirping sound.

"Here they come!" cried Elmer. "Those awful birds are going to eat the seeds!"

As soon as the birds saw the flamingos they squawked in surprise and flew away.

"They've gone!" said Elmer. "The pink flamingos scared them!"

"Exactly what I thought would happen," said Bugs.

"Bugs," said Elmer, "I don't know how to thank you.
You've saved my vegetable garden."

"Now we'll have corn on the cob for our picnics," said
Porky.

"And carrots," said Bugs. "Don't *ever* forget the carrots!"